The Littlest Shamrock

Sheredith Boore Heitzenrater
Author and Illustrator

To
Ezra

God Bless You
Sheredith Boore Heitzenrater
— 2020 —

The Littlest Shamrock

~Sheredith Boore Heitzenrater~
Author & Illustrator

Managing Editors: Travis Heitzenrater &
Jody Nichols Heitzenrater

Creative Editor: Tonia Heitzenrater Rouse

IBSN 978-1482502640

Published By CreateSpace, a dba of On-Demand Publishing, LLC,
an Amazon.comTM Company

Available on line
Printed in the USA

The Littlest Shamrock is dedicated to the
Glory of God,
and in Thanksgiving for all our many blessings.

Psalm 139:16
"Even before I was born,
You had written in your book everything I would do."

Long ago, in a meadow in Ireland, there lived a small family of clover.

MOM   JR   DAD

2

The Mother Clover looked
down at her little one.
He was twitching, twisting,
bending, stretching and
fluffing his three leaves.

4

Father Clover looked to the sky to see if there was a problem. All he saw were fluffy clouds that let in the warm sunshine. There was no rain in sight. No wind was blowing. Why was the little one twitching so?

Mother Clover asked,
"Little one, why can't you
stand still?"

"I'm trying to grow another leaf," said the little one. "All of my cousins have four leaves and I only have three," he sighed.

10

"Oh," said Mother Clover.
"That is how God made us."

"But they are so special,"
he wailed.
"Everyone wants to pick
one of them.
They never pick us."

14

"Don't worry," said Father Clover. "God made us this way for a reason. We just don't know what that reason is. We need to be patient."

The little one had trouble being patient. He still twitched and twittered while he watched his cousins get picked.

One four-leaf clover was picked by a little girl who wanted to put it in her dolly's hair.

20

One four-leaf clover was plucked by a boy who planned to make a bookmark with it. The clover would mark his reading spot in his favorite book.

One man selected a four-leaf clover, which he knew stood for faith, hope, love and luck. He planned to have it made into a necklace for his wife.

Hope   *Love*

Faith   *Luck*

The little three-leaf clover
just kept stretching and
growing. Some days the
warm sun smiled down
on them.

26

Some days the rain washed away the dirt on their leaves.

Some days the wind blew
so fiercely that the clover
almost lay completely down
in the grass.

People continued to pick
the four-leaf clovers.
The three-leaf young one
was very sad.

One day a British priest,
named Patrick, took a stroll
in the Irish meadow.
He looked through all the
clover till he found the
three-leaf family.
"Perfect", he thought,
as he picked them.

The priest took them to
the altar at the church and
began his sermon. He called
the clover "Shamrocks".
It came from an old Irish
word "seamrog". Seamrog
meant "little clover".

36

Saint Patrick preached to the congregation that they should always remember God as the "Trinity" – or three, like the three leaves on the shamrock.

38

One leaf is for
God, the Father.
One leaf represents
Jesus, the Son.
The third leaf is for the
Holy Spirit.

Son

Father   Holy
Spirit

From that day on the
three-leaf clovers were
known as Shamrocks.
They stood for the
Father, Son, and Holy Spirit.

Son

Father

Holy Spirit

42

March 17th is celebrated as
St. Patrick's Day.
The shamrocks help all
Christians celebrate their
basic beliefs. This made the
little clover very happy!

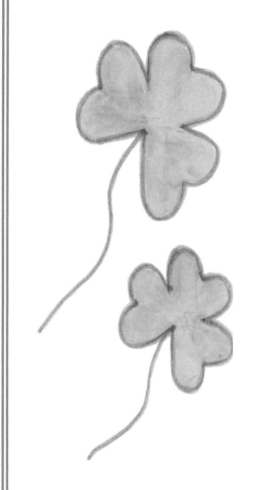

Remember:
No matter how
big,
No matter how
small,
God has a great
plan
For us all!

An Old Irish Blessing

May the road rise up to meet you.
May the wind be always at your back.
May the sun shine warm on your face,
And rains fall soft upon your fields,
And until we meet again,
May God hold you in the palm of
His hand.

AMEN!